THE ALWAYS PRAYER SHAWL

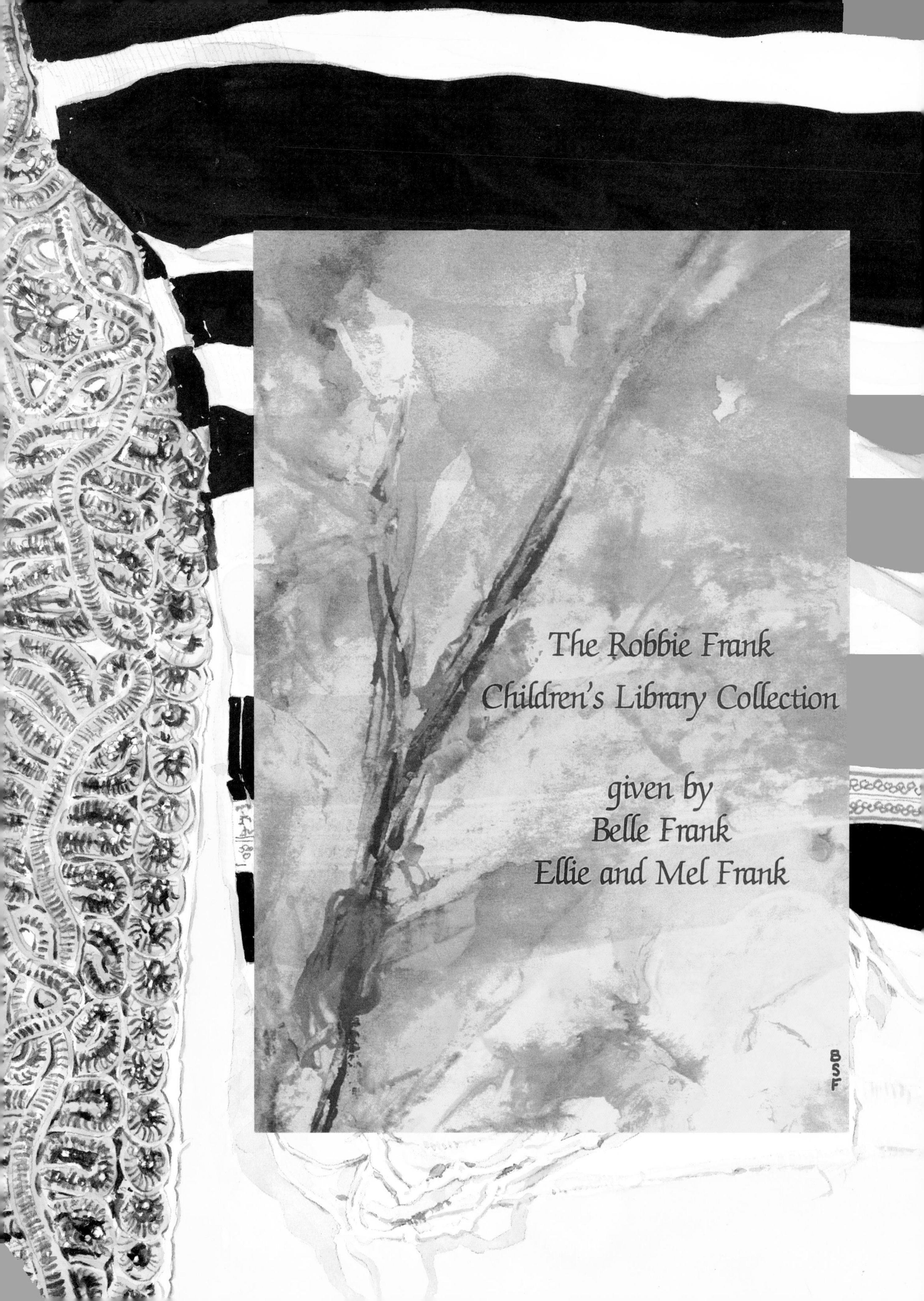
BSF

To my grandfather, Morris Stein,
and my son, Adam Morrison Oberman.

—S.O.

To my father's father, whom I never knew.

—T.L.

PUFFIN BOOKS
Published by the Penguin Group
Penguin Books USA Inc., 375 Hudson Street, New York, New York 10014, U.S.A.
Penguin Books Ltd, 27 Wrights Lane, London W8 5TZ, England
Penguin Books Australia Ltd, Ringwood, Victoria, Australia
Penguin Books Canada Ltd, 10 Alcorn Avenue, Toronto, Ontario, Canada M4V 3B2
Penguin Books (N.Z.) Ltd, 182-190 Wairau Road, Auckland 10, New Zealand

Penguin Books Ltd, Registered Offices: Harmondsworth, Middlesex, England

First published in the United States of America by Caroline House,
Boyds Mills Press, Inc., 1994
Published in Puffin Books, 1997
10 9 8 7 6 5 4 3 2 1

LIBRARY OF CONGRESS CATALOGING-IN-PUBLICATION DATA

Oberman, Sheldon.
The always prayer shawl / by Sheldon Oberman; illustrated by Ted Lewin.
p. cm.
Summary: A prayer shawl is handed down from grandfather to grandson in this story of Jewish tradition and the passage of generations.
ISBN 0-14-056157-9
[1. Jews—Fiction. 2. Grandfathers—Fiction. 3. Emigration and immigration—Fiction. 4. Tallith—Fiction.] I. Lewin, Ted, ill. II. Title.
[PZ7.01242Al 1997] [E]—dc20 96-33627 CIP AC

Printed in the United States of America
Set in 14.5 point Americana

THE ALWAYS PRAYER SHAWL

by Sheldon Oberman

illustrated by Ted Lewin

PUFFIN BOOKS

Adam was a Jewish boy in Russia many years ago.
When Adam went for eggs, he did not get them from a store.
He got them from a chicken.

When Adam felt cold, he did not turn a dial for heat.
He chopped wood for a fire.
When Adam went to town, he did not ride in a car.
He rode in a wagon pulled by a horse.

Adam did not go to a big school.
He went to his grandfather's house.
There his grandfather taught all the children
the stories of their people
and how to read and write in Hebrew.
All this was special to Adam,
but most special of all was Adam's name.

One day Adam asked his grandfather, "Why is my name Adam?"
His grandfather rubbed his beard and smiled.
He took Adam to the synagogue, and they sat by the window.
Adam shut his eyes and felt the warm sun
shining on his face.

Then his grandfather answered, "You are named after my
grandfather whose name was Adam. He was named after
his grandfather's grandfather whose name was Adam.
That way there will always be an Adam."

Adam laughed and whispered into his grandfather's ear,
"I am always Adam. That won't change!"
"Aha!" said his grandfather. "Some things change.
And some things don't."

Then many things began to change.
There was trouble in Russia.
There was not enough food. People were hungry.
Soldiers were fighting everywhere. Everyone was afraid.

Adam's parents said, "We must leave our home and go to a better place. It is so far away that we can never come back."

Adam's grandfather said, "You must go without me. I am too old to change anymore."

Adam cried, "I don't want to leave you, Grandfather! I will never see you again!"

Adam's grandfather kissed him for the last time.
He held out his prayer shawl and he said,
"My grandfather gave me this prayer shawl.
Now I am giving it to you."
Adam held it tightly against his chest.
He could hardly speak for his tears, so he whispered,
"I am always Adam and this is my always prayer shawl.
That won't change."

Off they went. Adam and his family traveled for weeks. They came to a town by the sea and got on a ship and sailed for weeks.

They came to a new country where everyone spoke a different language and wore different clothes.

Things changed even more. They moved into a small apartment in a big city. Adam's parents went to work in a factory. Adam went to school and learned English, science, and history.

Everything felt different except for the prayer shawl. Every Saturday Adam put on the prayer shawl and he said, "I am always Adam and this is my Always Prayer Shawl. That won't change."

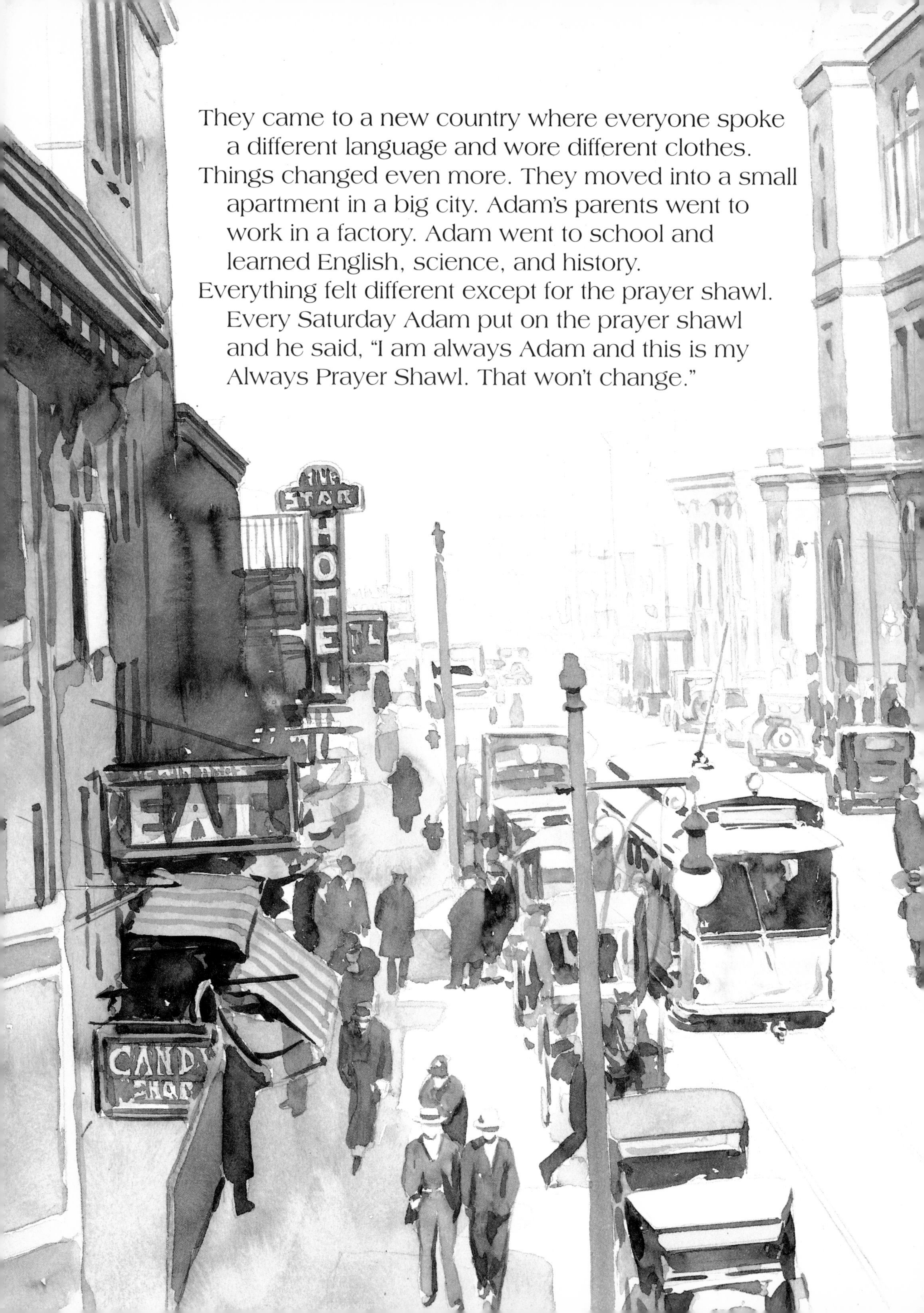

FOOD SHOP

Other things kept changing. Adam grew up and he married.
He worked in a store from morning until night.
Still, every Saturday Adam put on his prayer shawl.
Finally, the fringes wore out. So he sewed on new ones.

Then Adam had children. He moved to a house at the edge of the city. He drove back each day to work in an office. Still, every Saturday Adam put on his prayer shawl. Finally, the collar wore out. So he sewed on a new one.

Then Adam's children grew up. They moved out.
They married and had children of their own.
Adam and his wife grew very old, and they went to live in a home with other old people.
Still, every Saturday Adam put on his prayer shawl.
Finally, the cloth wore out. So he sewed on a new one.

One day, Adam's grandson came to visit.
"Grandfather," the grandson asked,
"Were you ever a kid like me?"
Adam rubbed his beard and smiled.
He said, "I was like you and I was not like you.
I got eggs from a chicken, not from a store.
I chopped wood for heat, I did not turn a dial.
I rode in a wagon pulled by a horse, and not in a car.
And I didn't go to a big school. I went to a little house
where my grandfather taught me many things."

The grandson asked, "What did he teach you?"
Adam took out his prayer shawl. He said, "Put this on. Maybe I can teach you something that he taught me."
Adam's grandson put on the prayer shawl.

They went to the synagogue, and they sat by the window.
They shut their eyes and felt the warm sun
shining on their faces.

Adam said, "This prayer shawl belonged to my grandfather.
Before that, it belonged to his grandfather whose name was also Adam. Now it is mine. And someday I will give it to you.
It has changed many times. The fringes changed.
The collar changed. The cloth changed.
Everything about it has changed.
But it is still my Always Prayer Shawl.
It is just like me. I have changed and changed and changed. But I am still Adam."

Adam's grandson whispered into his ear,
"I am going to be just like you. I will have a grandson whose name will be Adam. And someday I will give him this Always Prayer Shawl."

"Aha!" said Adam. "Now I can teach you something that my grandfather taught me. He taught me that some things change and some things don't."